ABOUT THE BOOK

From the Stone Age to the 18th century, the Australian Aboriginals existed in an isolated and virtually unchanged environment. Precisely where the Aboriginals came from is not known, but we do know that their ancestors settled in Australia 30,000 years ago.

The Aboriginals demonstrated the ability to live successfully in the varied environments of Australia—in deserts, in mountains, or along the seacoasts. They explored the environment, tested types of shelter, and learned the properties of plants and the habits of animals. And there were many times for sharing, cooperation and enjoyment of life.

In the 18th century Australia was invaded by peoples from another world in time. The invader and invaded were faced with many differences—differences in behavior, appearance, material traits, religious beliefs. After 200 years the awareness of these differences still challenges these two peoples to arrive at a mutual understanding. The perception of their greater human similarities is often obscured.

As you read Beyond Dreamtime, explore all the similarities to be found between our culture and that of the Aboriginals. Compare our native myths and folklore, and the experiences of the Europeans that settled our continent, with those of the Aboriginals. Understanding and accepting other cultures may allow us to achieve the one, encompassing world we all will need if we are to survive the future.

—Margaret Farrington Bartlett, General Editor

BEYOND DREAMTIME
The Life and Lore
of the Aboriginal Australian

by Trudie MacDougall

illustrated by Pat Cummings

Coward, McCann & Geoghegan, Inc. / New York

Library of Congress Cataloging in Publication Data
MacDougall, Trudie.
Beyond dreamtime.
SUMMARY: Introduces the history and cultural traditions of the Australian
Aboriginals, discusses the influence of the white man on their way of life, and
relates Aboriginal myths of the Dreamtime.
1.   Australian aborigines—Juvenile literature.   [1.   Australian
aborigines.   2.   Australian aborigines—Legends]   I.   Cummings, Pat.
II.   Title.   GN665.M214   994'.004'991   77-13944
Printed in the United States of America

This book was designed by Pat Cummings. The text type is set in Korinna
and the display type is set in Carlton. The black and white halftone art was
drawn with ebony pencil. The book was printed by offset on Troy Book
cream white paper at Westbrook Litho.

CONTENTS

JAVA

AUSTRALIA

N
W · E
S

INTRODUCING THE ABORIGINALS

It is believed the Aboriginals of Australia came to that land over thirty thousand years ago from the north. Some scientists think they came through Java, an island of Indonesia.

How had the Aboriginals lived?

No one knows.

What did they bring with them?

The only things anyone knows about are the dogs they brought, called dingos.

Archeologists are still digging and searching ancient campsites to learn more about these people.

Coming in some kind of watercraft, the Aboriginals settled in the northern part of Australia, where it was warm with plentiful rainfall. The seacoasts, rivers, and lagoons provided abundant fish and birds for food.

When the numbers of Aboriginals continued to increase, it was necessary for some of them to find new food-gathering areas and hunting grounds. Groups moved and spread all over this very large island, Australia. Some went to the dry, desert area, where there was space but less food. Others went westward, where mountains, rocks, and caves provided good hunting ground for kangaroos, wallabies, and large birds called emus. Aboriginals who went to the south, farther from the equator, found a colder climate where shelters and animal skins were needed for warmth.

When the Aboriginals reached Australia there were none of the wild animals found in other countries of the world—no lions, leopards, elephants, or deer. There were no domestic animals such as sheep, cows, or pigs.

What did they find?

They discovered most unusual animals: marsupials, the mammals that carry their young in pouches on their bellies. They found many marsupials, from tiny mice to giant kangaroos. While a few marsupial animals are found in other places, none of the ones in Australia are found anywhere else in the world, and they were new to the Aboriginals.

In the new world, the Aboriginals had everything to learn to stay alive.

They watched and listened. They smelled and tasted. They learned to make the tools and weapons they needed to live in this strange land.

9

Women must have something with which to dig vegetables, and so they made coolamons, curved wooden bowls. They dug and carried vegetables in these. A coolamon could carry water, seeds, or even a baby.

Some women wove dilly bags, deep baskets to carry food.

Flat stones and pebbles were used to grind seed into flour.

Stones were skillfully chipped to cut and carve wood and to make weapons.

Men made spears and spear-throwers out of wood to hunt and fish.

Some Aboriginal tribes made shields and boomerangs; others made dugout canoes.

The Aboriginals watched the stars, and by their movement and place in the sky learned when to expect the rainy, the dry, the hot or cold seasons. They made calendars in their minds.

When they heard the river pigeons' call, they knew the barramundi fish were going upstream.

The blooming of certain flowers told them of a special migration: geese coming to the swamps to eat water-lily bulbs.

When the blossoms of the corkwood trees turned red, the Aboriginals knew the yams, sweet potatoes, were ready to dig.

Thus the Aboriginals learned when and where to find certain foods.

The Aboriginals were the only people in Australia for tens of thousands of years—until Europeans began to settle there in 1788.

This book has stories and myths that tell about the life and adventures of Aboriginals in three different parts of Australia before the Europeans came.

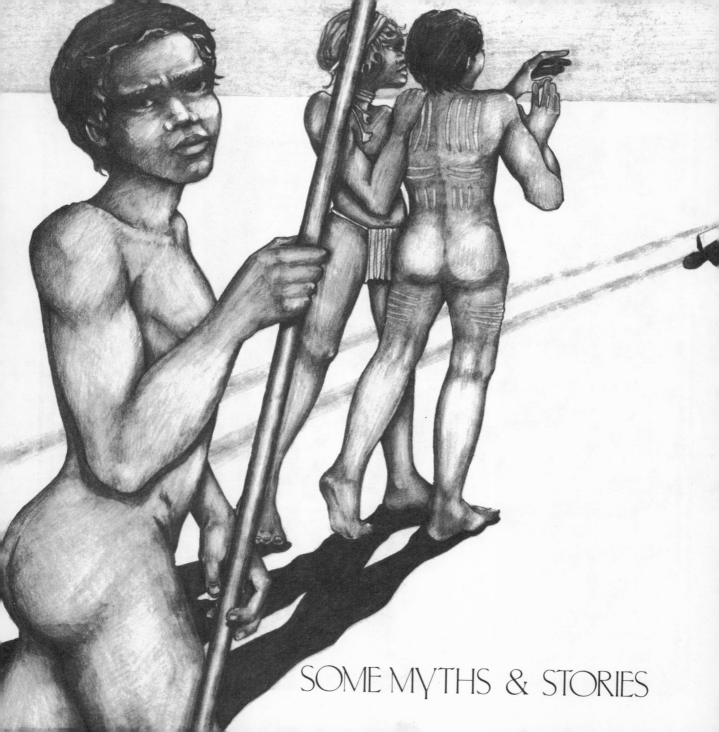

SOME MYTHS & STORIES

In the Beginning

How did the world begin?

The Aboriginals thought the earth was flat, a huge plain without animals, people, mountains, or rivers.

Then came Dreamtime, when giant semihuman beings arose and wandered over the entire land, making paths from one tribal land to another. They made fire, camped, searched for food, performed ceremonies, laughed, and quarreled like the Aboriginals of later years.

Then something mysterious happened.

Dreamtime came to an end.

These beings, who were believed to have great powers, changed the world. The places where they had performed special tasks became rivers and valleys. Great mountains arose, forests and jungles grew. These creatures changed themselves into plants and animals, thus creating a whole new world.

13

Everything in the new world was related to the Aboriginals' ancestors, and so the Aboriginals respected everything that lived or grew there. All around were the spirits of their ancestors—here, and everywhere: in the sky, on the earth, and below the ground.

All along the paths made by the ancestors were sites where something important had happened. Many a site was sacred and secret. Only a few of the wise elders knew the story of the happening, and they dared not tell woman or child. The punishment could be death.

All the Aboriginals believed in Dreamtime, but various tribes had their own special myths that told of the lives and adventures of their own ancestors. These myths explained the world to them. They told about the creatures that gave them food, about wind, rain, and thunder. There were many myths about the sun, the stars—the Seven Sisters, the Milky Way. Some tribes thought the thousands of stars were the flickering fires at the campsites of the sky people.

The Southern Cross

This myth says that the stars of the Southern Cross are a man Mululu and his four daughters.*

Mululu, the leader of a tribe, had four beautiful daughters, but no son. He was very fond of his daughters, but disappointed to have no son.

One day, when he was old, he brought his daughters together to tell them he was going to die. He told them that since they had no brother to protect them from having to marry a man they disliked, he wanted them to leave the earth when he died and to meet him in the sky. He told them a very clever medicine man, Conduk, would help them reach their new home. When their father died, the daughters started out to find Conduk. His camp was far to the north, and they had to travel many days to find him. Their father had described Conduk as having a long, thick beard, and so it was easy for them to recognize him when they finally found him resting in his camp. Beside him was a huge pile of silvery rope which Conduk had braided from the long hairs of his beard. One end of the rope reached up into the sky.

* The American flag has fifty stars representing the states. The Australian flag has four stars representing the Southern Cross, one of the brightest constellations. The Aboriginals think of these stars as the four daughters. Nearby in the sky is the very bright star Centaurus, which the Aboriginals think of as Mululu.

The girls were astonished and frightened when they realized the rope was the only way they could reach their father. But Conduk encouraged them and with his help they climbed and climbed until they reached the top of the rope. To their delight they found their father waiting for them.

Now, the daughters are four bright stars. Nearby is their father who cares for them.

Kuggun, The Bee Girl, and Vamar

In the Dreamtime there was no honey stored by the bees—only a sweet flower, the Manjil. One day a Bee girl named Kuggun came to a billabong, a waterhole. It was a sacred place, and when she went into the water to pick a beautiful red flower to suck the sweetness, a man yelled, "Hey, you, what are you doing in my Warragun, my sacred place?"

Kuggun was frightened. She knew it was serious to go into a sacred place. She might be killed.

Kuggun jumped out of the billabong to run away.

But the man, whose name was Vamar, caught her. "No, you can't go away. You are a girl and I will not kill you. You will be my wife."

"No, no, I don't want to live with you," she said. "Let me go."

"You will like it here. You will like my tucker," he said, meaning the food he ate, "and someday we will have children."

Vamar went into the bush to look for food, and when he returned he cooked Kuggun some lizards and snakes. "Eat this," he said, "it's good tucker."

"No," she said, going off to the billabong to find sweet flowers. This food was her tucker. She brought some to Vamar to taste.

"No," he yelled. "I don't want your tucker. You eat my tucker."

Vamar, filled with rage, went to the billabong and, pulling up all the flowers, threw them on the fire.

Kuggun was sad. "When we have children," she said, "they will eat my tucker, not yours."

Vamar laughed. "You'll see; I will show our children what to eat," he said.

Vamar and Kuggun lived together a long time and had many children. But as soon as a baby was born it changed itself into a bee and flew away in the bush.

There the bees lived together, making a swarm. Flying among the flowers, they took the sweetness and made it into a sugar bag for their mother, Kuggun.

Tiddalike, The Flood Maker

Tiddalike was thought to be the largest frog in the world. One morning he woke with a great thirst. He was so thirsty he drank and drank. He drank until all the fresh water of the world was gone. Plants and creatures began to die.

The other animals tried to think of something to do, but in vain. It was the old wombat who cleverly said, "Why not make Tiddalike laugh? Then all of the locked-up water will flow out of his mouth."

The animals decided to try this. The kookaburra bird told his funniest stories but only he laughed.

The kangaroo jumped over the huge emu.

No matter what they did, the frog looked glum and uninterested until finally the eel, Nabunum, stood on the tip of his tail and, feeling dry and uncomfortable, started to dance. He moved slowly at first and then as the dance got faster, he twisted himself into such funny shapes that Tiddalike burst out laughing. And as he laughed the water gushed forth from his mouth and flooded the land, filling all the dry lakes, swamps, and riverbeds.

The First Kangaroo

Thousands of years ago some Aboriginals were out hunting when suddenly a violent wind swept over the country. Trees were uprooted and everything that grew was torn from the ground. The Aboriginals ran to some caves for shelter and from there they watched the sky filled with swirling trees. The hunters were amazed to see animals being carried into the air by the fierce wind.

These animals had small heads, small forearms, large bodies and long hind legs, and long tails. Each time an animal tried to land on the

ground it was swept into the air again. But when there was a quiet break in the storm, the Aboriginals saw an animal fall to the ground and hop away. This was the first kangaroo.

When the hunters returned to the campsite they told their tribesmen what had happened. These people knew such a giant animal would provide food for many people. And so they all moved to the place where the kangaroo had fallen.

It took the Aboriginals a long time to learn how to capture kangaroos, the largest and swiftest animals of Australia.

THE DESERT PEOPLE

Meekadarriby and Yoodalong

There was laughter in the camp. The fires had burned low and people were stirring from their sleep.

This group of Aboriginal families consisted of desert people who had no dwellings. They slept in the open under the stars, each person near a small fire. They chose a campsite near a waterhole, and each night they returned to this spot. When there was no more food to forage they moved to another campsite.

Every day, desert families had to search for food. This morning the older boys gathered their clubs and throwing sticks and set forth to hunt for small animals—goannas, lizards, and snakes. The men had gone to hunt the larger animals—kangaroos and wallabies—with their long spears.

The women and children collected their dilly bags, digging sticks, and wooden bowls and started down the familiar path. They were chattering and laughing, but all eyes were on the ground looking for animal tracks and other signs of food.

Meekadarriby was a merry girl with dark brown sparkling eyes. She was loved by everyone, most of all by her younger sister Yoodalong. Sometimes they went with the women and children, but today they started alone in search of food.

Carrying only empty coolamons and digging sticks, the girls moved freely and happily, their naked brown skin gleaming in the early desert sunlight. They talked and joked, but they watched carefully for familiar marks in the sand. They saw tracks, but they were old ones. When Meekadarriby recognized some fresh ones she motioned Yoodalong to be quiet. They made signs with their hands, their eyes twinkling as they sent silent messages to each other.

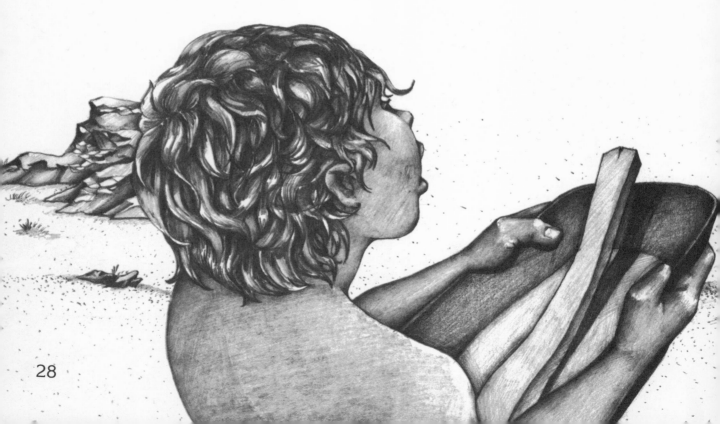

29

Suddenly Meekadarriby stopped and started to dig. She dug faster and faster to catch a lizard swimming away through the sand. She sprang and caught it—then Yoodalong caught one, and another and another. This was good food to share. Walking along, they gathered berries and grass seed. They dug yams, being careful to leave part of the tendril so the plant would grow again.

Yoodalong started to run and Meekadarriby followed. They had spied honey-ant hills. They dug and dug with their sticks, and finally they saw the underground nest of the ants, with dozens of tiny honey pots hanging from the ceiling, the honey stored in the abdomens of some of the ants. Meekadarriby and Yoodalong enjoyed tasting the wonderful sweetness.

Under the midday sun their feet began to feel the scorching sand. They were happy when they came to a large eucalyptus tree with spreading branches, and they rested under this big green umbrella eating the berries they had found.

Soon they were joined by women and children, the boys with witchetty grubs they had dug near the roots of a tree.

After resting they all moved along in the desert heat, small children riding on their mothers' shoulders, hanging on to their long, dark, wavy hair. A baby slept in a coolamon covered with leaves to protect him from the sun.

They hoped to find water soon. Meekadarriby hurried ahead, thinking she knew where there was a billabong. She stopped and then she told them the hole was dry. Everyone was disappointed but soon they moved on, too hot to talk, too thirsty to joke.

There was a sudden shout and happy laughter. Yoodalong had found a shallow pond filled with water from a passing rain. Everyone ran and fell into the water with great relief. Squealing, they splashed and rolled in the water.

They played a long time and then started back to camp. It was a long walk but the wetness of their naked skin cooled them.

Meekadarriby and Yoodalong gathered branches, skillfully carrying them on their heads. This evening when they reached camp they built a fence to protect them from the wind.

Some women started up the fires, others ground the grass seeds into flour and then with water made little cakes to toast in the fire.

Boys were cooking lizards over another fire. The men who had been hunting all day for a kangaroo or wallaby would soon return. Everyone hoped one of the hunters had speared a large animal, but this seldom happened.

These animals were scarce and hunting was difficult in such an open area.

The men depended on the women and children for their daily food.

MOUNTAIN COUNTRY

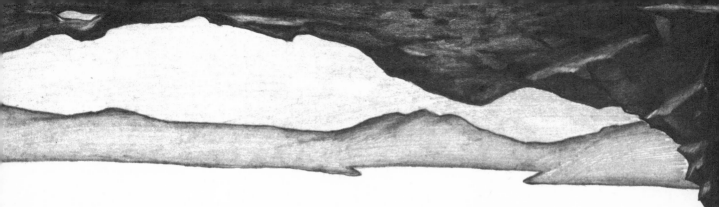

Killangoot and the Kangaroo Hunt

Killangoot and his family lived with other Aboriginal families in the western part of Australia, where there were rough mountains, hills, great rocks, and mammoth caves.

Killangoot was excited because at last he was going to hunt for a kangaroo with the men. Great skill is needed to capture a kangaroo, since it is such a clever animal. It can detect the slightest sound and escape with great hops at tremendous speed. Boys might make a move or a sound to frighten the animal, and so were not allowed to hunt with the men. But Killangoot's father felt his son was ready, for the boy had proved himself to be a good hunter of small animals.

Killangoot watched his father rub mud all over himself to cover his scent and to be less visible to animals. Only his father—the leader—did this. Then off they went, the men carrying spear-throwers and great long spears. They were joking and laughing but now, approaching a rocky section, Killangoot's father gave a signal for quiet. He held a branch in one hand, to look like a tree, and his spear in the other hand. He moved very very slowly because this was kangaroo country.

Suddenly he froze.

Everyone stood still.

Not a sound. Not a move.

All eyes searched the red rocks for kangaroos. But only Killangoot's father had seen him. Then, one by one, the men spotted a huge rusty-red kangaroo. Killangoot spotted the animal and almost yelled out with excitement. When the kangaroo began to eat, Killangoot's father moved again silently, slowly—one step, then another. He raised his long spear, poised to kill. He stopped, stood still. He moved closer, and when the kangaroo stopped eating he froze. He waited for the animal to start eating again. Then he raised his spear to strike. Suddenly he hurled it with deadly aim. It plunged into the kangaroo. The animal crumpled to the ground. There were shouts of excitement. Killangoot was proud of his father. He watched him bend the kangaroo's body and tie its hind legs. Then his father threw the huge animal around his neck and set forth for the return journey to camp.

Happy and excited, Killangoot and the men followed. The men had told Killangoot about the caves, and on the return journey they took him into a very large one to see the beautiful paintings on the walls. Generation after generation of Aboriginals had painted fresh pictures over the old ones to honor their ancestral heroes. The painting Killangoot liked best was a great red kangaroo painted over some large white figures.

The men explained that there were other paintings in certain caves, but these told a secret story and only a few of the wise elders could visit these picture galleries.

They followed Killangoot's father, and when they finally approached the camp they smelled the fires prepared by the women. This night there would be a feast.

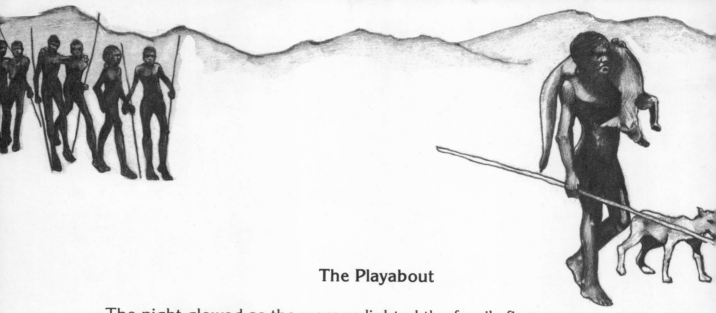

The Playabout

The night glowed as the women lighted the family fires with the smoldering fire stick. Elder men, too old to hunt, enjoyed joking and playing with the little ones.

Suddenly they heard the excited voices of the men returning from the hunt. Killangoot's father came first. He strode into the firelight tall and proud, the great kangaroo on his shoulders. Everyone crowded around him, astonished at the size of the animal.

Quickly the women began to prepare for the feast. They dug a shallow trench, filling it with branches, then lighting them with the fire stick. When the fire had burned down, several women lowered the gigantic animal into the glowing coals. It was on its back with its four feet in the air. They covered it with hot ashes and left it to bake.

Families sat around their fires, but the great elder men sat by themselves. They were the wise ones, the only men who knew the secret life of the tribe. A few of them were very old and were considered "close up dead." There was one head man who knew all the laws and customs. He presided at meetings and helped to settle quarrels.

Tonight they decided to have a Playabout for fun. The head man told the story of the kangaroo kill. He mimicked the successful hunter, exaggerating every move he had made. Everyone clapped and laughed.

Killangoot had been busy removing the skin of the kangaroo's tail, which his father had given him. He filled it tight with grass and sewed it with a bone needle and sinew. Tying the tail behind him, he made up a kangaroo dance with great fast hops around the fires. Everyone roared with laughter. A tall boy became the hunter, his spear poised to kill. Quietly and slowly approaching the kangaroo, he pretended to hurl his spear. Killangoot crumpled to the ground in a heap, and merry laughter rang out.

One of the girls strutted around the fires like a great emu. She bent her head and looked for bugs with one eye. Around and around the fires she walked a funny bird dance. Children wiggled along like snakes and hopped about like frogs.

Singing and dancing and laughter continued in the firelight until it was time to enjoy the delicious-smelling meat. The animal was taken out of the trench and cut up with sharp stones. Pieces were passed to the elders and then to the families of men, women, and children. Everyone ate with great relish and enjoyment—all but the great hunter. He ate very little. He watched the happy feast and was proud that he had provided this pleasure. To be the successful hunter was a great honor.

NORTH AUSTRALIA

Aberdan Goes Fishing

Aberdan lived with his family and a large group of related families in the northern part of Australia, by the sea. This area had islands. It was warm and tropical, with plentiful rain. There were rivers, lagoons, and swamps, and the seacoast which gave forth abundant food. Many kinds of birds—swans, pelicans, ducks, geese, gulls, and fairy penguins lived there. When the birds nested they were easily caught. The Aboriginals liked to gather birds' eggs to cook in the hot ashes of their fires. There were turtles, frogs, snakes and many kinds of fish.

It is no wonder so many Aboriginals chose to live in this part of Australia. There were many tribes, and though each one had a different language, the ones which lived close to each other could understand one another. Each tribe had its own territory, but people visited back and forth, and sometimes Aberdan's family invited people from another tribe to attend a ceremony.

These people of northern Australia had more permanent dwellings than desert people, because they needed protection from rain and they did not have to move often to find food. Their shelters were made with curved branches, with bark from the trees for roofing.

Some built huts on stilts, with fires underneath to keep mosquitoes away.

There was happy chattering and laughter in the camp this morning. Some of the older men were drawing in the earth, showing little children various tracks of animals and insects. Everyone laughed and patted the babies affectionately when a tiny one shouted the name of a familiar animal.

Some women were weaving dilly bags with colorful designs.

A few men were painting bark pictures for their own enjoyment, but most of the men preferred to paint Dreamtime heroes in order to keep the power of their spirits alive. Making permanent pictures was a way of recording their history.

Aberdan helped his father grind some yellow ocher between stones and mix it with oil from a swamp root. Pipe clay was used for white and charcoal for black.

Aberdan's father liked to paint on bark, and so he and his father had taken a sheet from a eucalyptus tree and flattened it over the heat of the fire, then placed it under stones.

After they removed the roughness, Aberdan's father started to paint with a brush made from stringy bark. He made white dots and lines, and within this frame painted a beautiful large yellow fish. "This is the fish we will catch when we go spearing," he said.

Aberdan's uncle was doing a kind of X-ray painting, a picture of a great serpent showing what he knew was inside—a backbone, lungs, and intestines, and other organs. He was drawing the story of mythical snakes that travel from place to place in the thunderclouds of the next

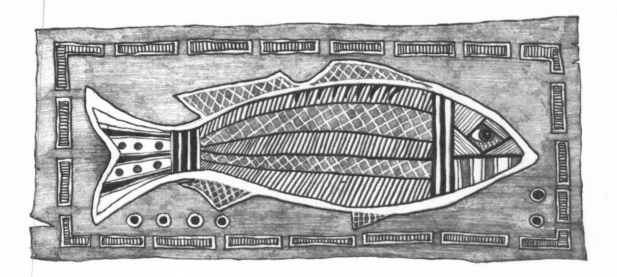

season. He skillfully painted spears to represent the lightning in the sky.

The next day Aberdan and his father went fishing in the bark canoe they had made, the father pushing the canoe with a long spear. It had a sharp kangaroo bone on the end to spear fish. His father stood in the canoe holding the spear in both hands, and Aberdan sat very still watching his father keep a delicate balance. He knew a sudden move or even a breath of air could upset them.

His father pushed against the water first on one side, then on the other. Then he stopped moving and threw a stick sharply into the bottom of the lagoon to disturb the fish. If there were any fish there they hurried and scurried in sudden fright moving the water plants.

Aberdan and his father sat still until the water plants stopped moving, and then his father silently pushed the canoe to the exact spot where he had thrown the stick. Suddenly he plunged his spear down where the fish were hiding. Up came a yellow quivering fish on the point of the spear.

Aberdan felt the magic of the bark painting had worked, and they returned to camp to show their catch.

Aberdan's Initiation

One day there was loud crying throughout the camp. Aberdan was being taken away from his family to a separate camp for youths, and his mother and other women took up spears to try to prevent his departure. They cried and they wailed. But they were only pretending, because they knew he must go. It was their custom.*

Now that Aberdan was fourteen years old his father and the great, wise elders had decided it was time for him to be initiated into the secret life of the tribe. Excited but a little afraid, Aberdan stood while the elders painted him with red ocher. Then, leaving the camp of children and wailing women with pointed spears, they started for the youth camp. On the way they invited other neighboring groups to come to the initiation ceremonies which would soon begin.

Aberdan was glad to find an old friend, Jingereat, at the camp. They would go food gathering together and talk about their feelings. The boys had looked forward to this great event of initiation all of their lives, but they worried about the pain and long discipline they knew would come.

Many groups arrived at the camp. It was understood that all old quarrels must be settled before this ceremony could start. Suddenly one group shouted angrily at another group, accusing it of wrongdoing. The

* All Aboriginal boys were initiated into the secret world of the elders, but the customs and ceremonies varied from one tribe to another.

51

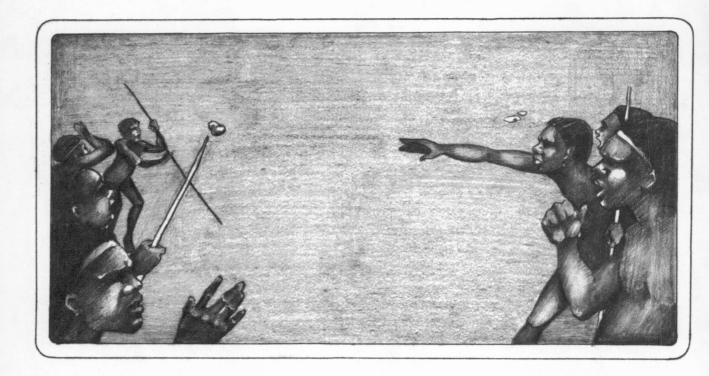

other shouted its answer and then its accusation. Angry words flew back and forth and then the weapons flew. Men were hit and there was blood on the ground. Suddenly the shouting and fighting stopped and the men apologized for hurting each other. Now that all arguments were settled, there was peace and then the ceremony was begun.

In the firelight with darkness all around, some of the elders made preparations for the corroboree.* They began to paint the bodies of the young initiates with red, black, and white colors. The wise elders painted with great care, using special designs and colors for this occasion.

* Singing, dancing, and acting, usually at night with sticks or a didjeridu, a hollo bamboo instrument. The stories might be secret, sacred, or everyday experiences.

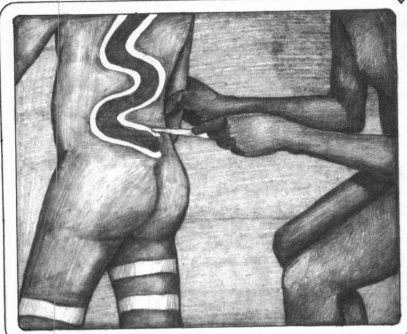

During this slow, quiet body painting one of the elders began to chant the story of the past. He stopped to explain each verse to the initiates. Aberdan and the other young men listened carefully to the many verses that united them with heroes of the past.

Now others were feeling the mood of this important event and joined in the singing and dancing. They stamped their feet to the rhythm of the stick beats. One elder played the didjeridu, blowing into it trumpet fashion.

The fires blazed and the painted bodies glowed in the firelight. The young men began to feel the tense emotion of the elders as they chanted the story that told about their ancestors and past heroes.

The dancing went on and on into the night, and when it stopped everyone felt reunited and uplifted in spirit.

The next morning the groups returned to their own campsites, but the boys remained with their guides. These men would teach the youths the tribe's secret code and language and assist them in other ceremonies.

During the weeks and months of the initiation period that followed, Aberdan and other youths were taken to many sacred grounds in the bush to learn more about the customs and beliefs of the tribe. When they were ready to see more of the symbols and rites of the secret life, there was another ceremony.

It was a tradition to knock out a front tooth of the initiates. An elder loosened Aberdan's front tooth with a twig and then he knocked it out, sending the tooth around to various groups to show how far Aberdan had advanced in the initiation rites.

After many months the elders decided it was time for the blood ceremony. Taking blood from their own arms, they gave some to Aberdan to drink. Chanting a special song, they drank the sacred blood themselves and anointed each other. This blood had a sacred name and was thought to give strength and courage to Aberdan and the other

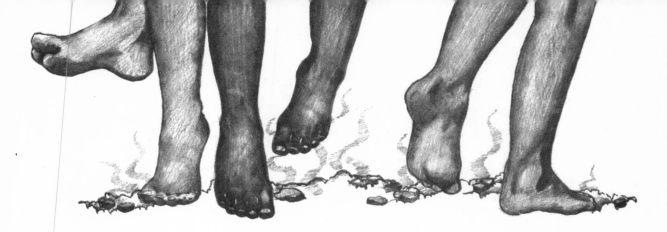

initiates. A special song was chanted. The boys listened attentively to the song that united them to heroes of the past.

Finally, after a long period of discipline, the elders prepared the final rite, the fire ceremony. They had built a tremendous blazing fire, and the initiates stared at it, almost dazed. When at last the fire burned down, they all trampled on it with their feet. The youths were amazed to see that the elders seemed to feel no pain. When they had stamped out the hot coals they did feel pain.

Now, after more than a year, the initiates were preparing to go back to their family camps. Before joining the uninitiated at their home site there was a washing ceremony to clean off the blood and other traces of the secret, sacred world.

Aberdan knew that he had gone through this part of the initiation well, and he was proud that he had taken a big step from boyhood to manhood. He would go on learning from the elders year after year. Aberdan was confident that he would marry, have children, and eventually be taken into the small group of elders who held the secrets of their ancestral heroes.

When Aberdan and the other youths returned to their family groups there was a great corroboree prepared by the women to welcome them.

YESTERDAY, TODAY & TOMORROW

The Aboriginals of Australia lived in harmony with nature, alone and undisturbed, for thousands of years.

When the first European settlers came to Australia in 1788 there were approximately 300,000 Aboriginals living there. Year after year great numbers of Europeans arrived, and before long they outnumbered the Aboriginals.

The Europeans brought new diseases with them to Australia. Smallpox and tuberculosis killed great numbers of Aboriginals.

The new settlers were different from the Aboriginals in customs, beliefs, language, and color.

The Europeans needed grazing land for their farm animals, so they used Aboriginal tribal land. With less tribal land there was less food for the Aboriginals. So the Aboriginals speared cattle and sheep and stole crops from the new settlers.

Clashes developed.

The Europeans used guns and many people were killed.

During these years the Europeans and Aboriginals had much to learn about each other's customs and beliefs.

Gradually the Aboriginals began to adjust to these new people in various ways. Some moved to the outback and farther north and tried to continue their own way of life.

Others lived near pastoral farms and worked as cattlemen.

Some worked in towns for the new settlers.

Many lived on reservations set aside for them by the Australian government.

But the Aboriginals who moved to towns missed their old ways of life. Their tribal territory was the home of their ancestors' spirits and of their own spirits before they were born. After death their spirits would be reborn to start a whole new cycle of life. This was their only assurance that life would continue.

The Aboriginals missed the familiar paths of their tribal land, the sacred sites along the paths.

They missed their corroborees.

Many who lived in towns insisted on sleeping out of doors under the familiar sky.

Some left the towns for short periods to return to their life in the open, free world of nature.

In recent years the Australian government and other interested people have worked with the 150,000 Aboriginals alive today to help them gain more independence and opportunities for a better life. In 1967 the people of Australia voted to include all Aboriginals as citizens of Australia.

The Aboriginals now have their own leaders to help them make decisions about their present and future life.

Now young people, descendants of Meekadarriby, Yoodalong, Aberdan, and others, have more choice deciding what they want their lives to be. They can help make the laws that govern them. Some are entering a new way of life, becoming nurses, ministers, artists, athletes, teachers, doctors, or leaders in their government.

Some are combining the old and new ways of living, but this is extremely difficult.

Many Aboriginals want to seek out the wise elders who can teach them their own history and help them find a way back to their tribal beliefs and customs. They may be able to do this to some extent, but they will never be able to go back to the food-gathering, hunting days of pre-European times.

Their traditional world has changed forever.

GLOSSARY

Billabong   Australian name for a water hole

Boomerang   curved, flat weapon made of wood which when thrown will return to the thrower; used for fighting or hunting

Coolamon   large wooden bowl

Corroboree   group celebration of singing and dancing; may include acting out everyday experiences; some corroborees have a sacred or mythological meaning

Didjeridu   musical instrument of bamboo wood, four or five feet long; produces a deep organlike note; used only in certain areas of Australia

Dilly bag   small or big basketlike bag woven from bark, string, or grass

Emu   large ostrichlike bird, approximately five feet tall; can run 40 miles an hour

Goanna   lizard found in Australia

Kangaroo   marsupial animal found only in Australia; there are many varieties, ranging from tiny to giant; all run by hopping on their hind legs

Playabout   camp gathering purely for fun; familiar animals are mimicked and everyday events are played out with song and dance

Tucker   Aboriginal word for food

Wallaby   small- and medium-sized kangaroo

Witchetty grub   large white grub, the larva of a moth

Wombat   stocky Australian marsupial which resembles a small bear

SUGGESTED READINGS

Most of these books have been written for adults to help them gain a better understanding of the Aboriginals of Australia. However, books marked with an asterisk (*) are ones which would interest younger readers, too. Although many of the titles published in Australia may not be available in all libraries throughout the United States, they are listed here because the inclusion of excellent photographic materials makes them a valuable resource for further information.

ABORIGINAL AND ISLANDER IDENTITY. Perth: The Aboriginal Publications Foundation, Vol. 2, No. 10, Oct., 1976.

* ABORIGINAL BARK PAINTINGS. Robert Edwards and Bruce Guerin. Adelaide: Rigby Ltd., 1969.

ABORIGINAL MYTHS. Sreten Bozic in conjunction with Alan Marshall. Hawthorn: Gold Star Publications, 1969.

ABORIGINES AND THEIR COUNTRY, THE. Charles P. Mountford. Adelaide: Rigby Ltd., 1969.

AN ATTEMPT TO EAT THE MOON. Deborah Buller-Murphy. Melbourne: Georgian House, 1958.

AUSTRALIAN ABORIGINAL ANTHROPOLOGY: Modern Studies in the Social Anthropology of Australian Aborigines. Edited by Ronald M. Berndt. Published for the Australian Institute of Aboriginal Studies by the University of Western Australia Press, 1970.

* AUSTRALIAN ABORIGINAL CULTURE. Australian National Commission for UNESCO. Canberra: Australian Government Publishing Service, 1973.

* AUSTRALIAN ABORIGINAL ROCK ART. Frederick D. McCarthy. Sydney: Published by Authority of the Trustees of the Australian Museum, 1967.

AUSTRALIAN ABORIGINALS. Canberra: Australian Government Publishing Service, 1974.

AUSTRALIAN ABORIGINES, THE. A. P. Elkin. 5th ed. Sydney: Angus and Robertson, 1974.

BEFORE THE WHITE MAN. Peter J. White. Sydney: Reader's Digest, 1974.

* BOY AND A GIRL, A: Legends of the Aborigines. Isabel Weir. Sydney: Reed.

BUSH FAMILIES OF TIDBINBILLA. Dorothy Braxton. Canberra: Australian Government Publishing Service, 1974.

CHANGE AND THE ABORIGINAL. Nicolas Peterson. Canberra: Australian Government Publishing Service, 1975. An educational pamphlet.

DESERT PEOPLE. M. Meggitt. Sydney: Angus and Robertson, 1974.

* DREAMTIME BOOK, THE: Australian Aboriginal Myths. Text by Charles P. Mountford. Paintings by Ainslie Roberts. Englewood Cliffs, N.J.: Prentice-Hall, 1973.

* ENCYCLOPEDIA OF ABORIGINAL LIFE. Sydney: Reed, 1974.

QUESTION OF HARMONY, A: The Relationship Between Australian Aboriginals and the Natural Environment. Canberra: Dept. of Aboriginal Affairs, 1976.

STUDIES IN AUSTRALIAN GEOGRAPHY. Edited by G. H. Dury and M. I. Logan. Melbourne: Heinemann Educational Australia, 1968.

THESE WERE MY TRIBESMEN. Alan Marshall. 3rd ed. Sydney: Rigby Ltd., 1965.

TIWI OF NORTH AUSTRALIA, THE. C. M. Hart and Arnold R. Pilling. New York: Holt, Rinehart and Winston, 1960.

WOMAN'S ROLE IN ABORIGINAL SOCIETY. Edited by Fay Gale. AAS 36. Australian Institute of Aboriginal Studies, 1974.

ABOUT THE AUTHOR

Trudie MacDougall is an inveterate traveler who has made several trips around the world. It was on one of her many visits to Australia that she first became interested in the fascinating culture of the Aboriginals and began formulating ideas for this book, her first juvenile title.

Holder of BS and MA degrees from Teachers College, Columbia University, the author was for many years a teacher at and the director of the Lower School at the Dalton Schools in New York City.

She and her husband, Hugh, now live in Connecticut where Trudie is involved in helping to run the Eliot Pratt Education Center, which she and her late husband, Eliot Pratt, started in 1968 on 170 acres of family land. The Center, a classroom without walls, helps children, teachers and adults enjoy, understand and appreciate their natural environment.

ABOUT THE ARTIST

Pat Cummings was born in Chicago, Illinois, but spent most of her childhood living all over the world. A graduate of Pratt Institute in Brooklyn, New York, Pat is currently involved in designing greeting cards, creating children's theater posters, and drawing magazine illustrations.

In addition to illustrating and designing <u>Beyond Dreamtime</u>, the artist has also illustrated <u>Good News</u> by Eloise Greenfield for Coward, McCann & Geoghegan.

She and her husband, Chuku Emeka Lee, live in New York City.